A

Life

In

Verse

 The author is also available for speaking engagements and may be contacted via email at authortonihenry@gmail.com.

Manufactured in the United States of America

ISBN-13: 979-8-218-03634-8

FIRST EDITION

Book Cover Design: Toni Henry

Executed by: Kozakura

Editor: WesCourt Advisors

A Life in Verse

Toni Henry

DEDICATION

This book is dedicated to

all the ladies, femmes, goddesses, females,

. . . everyone,

not willing to settle for anything less than love and butterflies.

ACKNOWLEDGEMENTS

This book chronicles my life experiences, heartaches, and perseverance with some embellishment.

To Natasha Wilson Green, thank you for your outreach to assist me with publishing my book. Your effort was the catalyst in the completion of its publication. Thank you to editors Tuesday White and Sheila E. Fleming for refining my story. Much gratitude is given to Kozakura at Fiverr for being able to execute my vision for the book jacket. Thank you for helping me to publish this book and to allow me to share my personal journey through poetry.

A heartfelt shout out is given to Marco Hurt, my longest and dearest friend. Thank you for being my road dog , and for picking up with me after I returned from my "*mid-life crisis*". Thank you to Jeffrey Bellamy and Michael Levy for being great friends, for always giving me an ear and for the laughs and good times. To all the musical artists who sang me through my joys and pains and let me know that I wasn't alone in this journey, thank you.

Preface

My initial intention was not to write a book. I simply wrote when I felt - deeply. The first poem was written after my first heartache at the age of seventeen. I cried for an hour and a half, and later realized that I had used up all my tears. I continued to write for over two decades. I was mostly motivated to write when I was either agitated or pensive about life; therefore, the poems convey a range of life experiences from melancholy to hopeful, sexual, and triumphant. Realizing that lessons could be learned from my poetry, I then sought to publish my journey to help guide the young, and the naive, to reassure the hopeless romantic and those who feel like "*life's*" just happening to them. Ultimately, the book is intended for the general enjoyment of all.

Foreword

Ideally, the poems in this book should be read in order, as they tell a story. Some latter poems build on earlier poems, so read them in order to understand and appreciate the complete story. Then, revisit them, share your favorites, and reflect on the lessons learned through the experience.

You will find yourself within these pages by reliving a relationship or empathizing with the challenges and experiences of others. This book is an excellent tool to help navigate the roller coaster ride most will endure.

Table of Contents

Volume I

Epigraph

"Happiness is like a butterfly;
the more you chase it,
the more it will elude you,
but if you turn your attention to other things,
it will come
and sit softly on your shoulder."

- *Henry David Thoreau*

VOLUME I

Prologue

"What comes from the heart, goes to the heart."

-Samuel Taylor Coleridge

My First

Love is like the wind.
It's known to be there
through sound and touch.
Yet to grasp it - is Impossible.
You can feel it Indefinitely,
but never capture it Forever.

Don't Hear Me - Listen

Could I stand naked before you
and you not make a move?

Could I stand naked before you
and you not say, "I love you"?

Could I stand naked before you
and you hear what I'm saying?

Could I stand naked before you
and you hear what I'm saying?

Could I stand naked before you
and you know the color of my eyes?

Could I stand naked before you?

True Love

Stumbling upon one another and
discovering things, Brand New.
Feeling emotions for the first time.
Taking up each other's every moment and loving it.
Taking vigil of his sleep and
slyly watching her shower.
Smiling and laughing all the time,
Cuddling up together, watching the same movie for the
fifth time.

Misunderstandings
Unfounded Jealousy
Arguments over nonsense, only because you care.
Familiarity breeding contempt
Distance taking the place of affection
Passion taking the place of love.

Unintentional Hurt
Growing Apart
Letting Pride get in the Way
Breaking Up
Being Hurt

Losing Friendship or realizing there never was one.
To Abhor ...but there's always that thin line.
Losing Touch.

Being able to, after time - call to just shoot the breeze,
and recapture some of those special times.
Possibly Rekindling an Old Romance
Or Just Becoming Friends, Maybe the Best Of.

A Coward's Way Out

You said, *"Bye"* in Silent Words
and left me in my solitude.
I sat in shock and could not cry.
I would not let you go.
And even though you found a new *'love'*
my love did not despair.

So, when you wake and come around
with open arms, I'll be here.

Sweet Nectar

For the Sake of Sweet Nectar,
he stole your heart.
But he took good time,
to make it worthwhile.

Sweet Nectar
what it makes men do.
It either makes boy - man
or reverts him to childhood.

Sweet Nectar
will do it every time.
It will make him fall in love,
or it will make him leave you
for Sweeter Nectar.

Sweet Nectar
it can even make the 'better half'
go astray.
For if yours can't bring you to that
'sacred place'
Sweet Nectar brought about by another,
has found a temporary space.

Daydreams

Daydreams are wishes,
and if dreams came true,
my eyes would remain closed,
so I'd always be with you.

It Don't Come Easy

I guess I'm being foolish
thinking you'd leave
- her that is.

I don't know why I set myself up.
I Did – but you are also to blame.

You put my defenses down and made me like you.
Then told me you were married
- so to speak.

Involved,
and baby makes three.
Why me?

I thought you were being honest – to shoo me away,
Not because you wanted me to stay.

My "No", was only temporary.
I tried, but you're…made for me.
What did I expect?

For me to let you go
Ideal, but this is reality
You are beautiful; not just what I can see, but how you make me feel.

What irony!
Honesty about being a cheat, a liar, a fink.

What flattery – all for me.
Even though I know your capabilities of doing the same to me.

I stayed.
And here we are happy and uncertain,
Wondering when you'll leave
 - me that is.

To be with your girlfriend, how it pains me to say.

Oh, what a life!
Is a Mistress all I'll ever be?
And she, soon and ever your wife?

The "F" Word

Look at where we are now,
friends.
This is where we should've started.

But like the humans we are,
we need instant gratification.

I can't believe the path we've taken
the rocky, dark, unpaved
back trail.

Sure, it gave us the excitement of intimacy,
but no direction at all.
Ceased was communication,
and we seemed to have gotten lost and separated.

Friends.
The infamous "F" word.
I'm glad we've found our niche.
We're on Main Street now.
and I expect a dip or a pothole unexpectedly.
But at least now my eyes are peered,
and my ears will take heed.

Who knows what may occur?

Parental Discretion is Advised

He's tall and brown and handsome
in his youthful way.

His eyes, so wide
I can see his innocence
hidden within this callous world.

His touch, so soft, like a child.

He bites his nails.
What's the matter?

His kisses, so ...perfect
Need I say more?

His heart so pure,
hidden behind a thick skin and a hard head.

His smile so sweet,
you can't help but love it.
It's sincere.
I can't help but forgive him.
He meant no harm.

He always requests, *"Gimme a Kiss"*.
He warms my heart.

My pictures remain where they were first placed,
on his shelf with his trophies.
Not to imply that I am one,
but I know he holds me in high regard.
And why not?
I'm an older woman.

He's my junior and not just by a few years.
But I care and I'm concerned
and don't get me wrong, I'm *very* strongly attracted.

But what's a girl to do,
Oh, excuse me, a lady - to do
with a child?
Oh, Don't Be Absurd!
He's legal.
Twenty and 5/12th to be exact.

How did it happen?
It just did.
His touch: gentle - curious,
Almost with fascination.

His passion,
he's engulfed, almost lost.

I like that.

My satisfaction
is his,
but I wouldn't mind more.

I don't know why I'm making
such a big deal.
There's no relationship,
but we're definitely involved.

I'm not afraid of losing him.
I just don't know how wise this is.
I want the best for him
and right now, that's me.

He's misdirected and unequipped.
If anyone could be able to,
I could help him to become a man,
no longer just a male.

I could probably make him all I ever wanted in a man.
(But should I – is that right?)

And I wouldn't mind if even then, he went his separate way,
just as long as I knew he'd be okay.

I Think.

I don't think I could ever feel scorned,
because I'm concerned, and it's all for his well-being.

But life is funny, and so is love.
So, there's a chance
that he might go astray,
or maybe I'll get bored.

But it would be nice, no perfect I suppose
if this was a fairy tale romance,
and we didn't end up foes.

You, Me, and Everybody Else

Model child.
You miss out on rebelling.

Angel.
Not really,
What They Don't Know Won't Hurt 'em.

Decisions.
Too many things I would do differently.

Parents.
Need I say More?

Lovers.
Come and go.

I'm Lonely.
So is everybody else.

Marriage.
The Ultimate Routine.

Looking back,
What a travesty.

Volume II

VOLUME II

Prologue

"If you love someone, set them free, if they come back they're yours; if they don't they never were."

-Richard Bach

Gambling

Dreams are hopes,
inner desires
of aspirations we plan for the future.

And when we plan dreams for love,
we set ourselves up for chances.
A chance that things will go wrong,
a chance for 50 – 50
and the littlest chance that everything
will fall right into place.

Simplicity

What I want in my life is one simple thing:
The sun on my skin,
A fast car to speed in.

To find a spot in the shade,
Find my niche and get paid.
A cozy mansion to rear a family,
A big backyard with a pool.
Sleek black statues,
Yeah, wouldn't that be cool.

One simple thing, that's all that I plea
a man who loves me dearly
and lets my heart run free.

Foreplay

I want to dance
in total darkness
with only the light of your eyes
to guide me.

I want to dance
in total silence
with only the sweet sexy sound
of your breath to soothe me.

I want to dance
with total freedom
with only your lean strong arms
to confine me,
to hold me close to my serenity
my sanity,
my peace of mind.

My You.

August 21st

It's a strange and peculiar feeling
That definitely out-shadows the rest.
It's a welcomed change from the usual,
My God, this could be the best!

Did you ever feel yourself falling in love?
Well, I think I can finally say yes.
I think I felt it happening
this past August 21st.

It was a day we did really nothing
but a little bit more than we ever did.
It involved deep looks into eyes
and soft kisses onto lips.
Hugs and embraces, as I lay my head upon his chest.

Did you ever feel yourself falling in love?
It's a feeling that comes with patience,
hopes, dreams - infinite.

It's a strange and peculiar feeling
from a situation that's not quite perfect.
But there are qualities, non-negotiable
that you wouldn't do without,
that bring you smiles and certainty
I believe I have no doubts.

Did you ever feel yourself falling in love?
Well, I think I can finally say yes.
I think I felt it happening
this past August 21st.

Silent Agony

Did you ever feel your heart breaking?
I think I feel an echo of it now.

It feels like uncertainty
Wrapped in feelings of betrayal,
disappointment, lost hopes, dreams, and efforts.
It's wondering where his heart is,
And why he hasn't thought to call.
It's the revelations that flood your mind
when you're sitting all alone.
It's realizing the unthinkable,
the worst joke of all:
that the house that was built for his heart
has found another home.

Did you ever feel numb inside?
That was because you were afraid to feel anything at all.

An Experience

Have you ever had your heart broken?
Trust me, you don't want to know
the feeling.

It's a numb, painless hurt
that has no other cure
but time.

You never know when you'll wake up
and not have that feeling
bring you down.

Did you ever get your heart broken?
It's an empty, hollow, hopeless situation.

It's a hurt that's unexplainable,
something you can't quite understand.
Unless you've stood in these here boots,
it's something you wouldn't
comprehend.

Well, I've had my heart broken once,
the other time, I can't deduce.
He left in silent words
and that's the painful truth.

No explanation, no reason
just a simple word, bye.
No kiss on the cheek,
no hug, no sigh.
No clue, no hint,
not a bit of evidence.

He left me in a silent trance.

Have you felt your heart breaking?
It's not at all what you might think.

It's a montage of dreams that will never come true.
It's hopes and aspirations that go right down the tubes.
It's a ceremony that gets cancelled
even before the invitations are thought about.
A house that won't get built,
children you'll never meet
A house that won't become a home,
it's a lonely, abandoned street.

Have you ever had your heart broken?
Well, I hope that you never do.
It's an experience that lasts a lifetime
each time it remembers you.

SUCH IS LIFE

What do I feel?
Nothing.
And sometimes I actually don't think too much.
I refuse.
I'll simply let it be a gradual recognition,
A slow internal death.
I'll stifle the feelings of insult,
Never allow it to muster into hurt.
I'll acknowledge it as dissatisfaction
And ignore the painful truth.

I brought this all on myself
And of course, he too is to blame.
I knew back then of his wide eyes
hard head, nail biting,
and perfect kisses.

He warmed my heart.

I ignored reason.
Oh, what the hell with logic!

Reality was no idealistic fantasy.
Frustration became my first name.
So, now what do I do
When I'm caught up in irony?
In, you know what I mean,
a circumstance of pure misery.

I'm truly trapped between that Oh, letting go',
Then waiting,
waiting for that butterfly to come sit softly on my
shoulder.

I'm wondering,
wondering if
that free someone would come back to me
and if so, would I really care?

But in my mind,
that forever-ticking bomb.
I know that you don't settle.
You don't hold on because you're afraid,
because all things do run their course
of a circle, yes, that 360 degrees
if it's truly meant to be.

AFFECTION

I'm not actually feeling like a cat,
a cat wound up on a hot tin roof.
But I'm definitely feeling lonely,
Lonely for that affection that is no more.

I miss having someone to love,
and I miss feeling loved.

I miss having someone to cuddle next to me
and fit my every bend with strong arms
to hold me close.

I miss having his neck to snug
my head in as I lay beside him with
my legs pinning him near.

I miss the sweet, soft kisses that
held me through the night and
welcomed me in the morning.

I miss him.

Sweet Bitterness

I still haven't yet, in all my travels,
found the true meaning of love.

What is it,
who is it,
how is it,
and why?

It's funny,
I've given it a chance
and taken that, oh big whirl,
and truthfully,
it's not for this little girl.

I like my freedom.
I want to spread my wings
with no strings to hold me back
from experiencing life's most wondrous things.

So, thanks for the bite.
I've had quite enough.
Simply, no thanks.
I've lost my appetite.

STRUGGLES

Ever were glad you did
something that at the
time, you found so hard
to do?
Well, I did.
Man, what was I getting into?

Loneliness.

Needs - Desires

No one to kiss, no one to hug
as I turn my back on this concept of love.

No one to touch, no one to feel
when I acknowledge that love couldn't possibly be real.

No one to hold, no one to caress
as I stand amongst this crowd of loneliness.

No one to admire, no one to adore
as I hang my head in sorrow as a tear hits the floor.

No one to listen, no one to hear
that to grow old alone is a terrible fear.

No one's heart, no one's soul
to raise my spirit when I return home.

Realizations

Letting it go
like water as it seeps through your fingers
as your hands elevate in the air.

Letting it go
as the brisk winds caress your head
beneath your hair.

Letting it go
as the sun sinks beneath the horizon
awaiting a new day.

Letting it go.
when you can finally breathe
deep without a sigh.

Letting it go.
as the midnight ceiling wraps the unending sky
as memories fade and sail on *bye.*

FYI

When a man loves a woman,
she's his first thought in the morning,
the last thought before his slumber,
and a million thoughts in between.

When a man loves a woman,
he'll do anything to please her.
Pleasing her, pleases him,
and he couldn't be happier to see her pleased.

When a man loves a woman,
he listens when she speaks.
He doesn't just hear her,
he thinks about what she's said.

When a man loves a woman,
he doesn't forget to call.
He's motivated by love just to hear her voice.

When a man loves a woman,
he's truly concerned about her feelings,

and when she talks to him, he's never at a loss for words
because his heart always tells him what to say.

When a man loves a woman,
it's because he's learned to love himself.

Volume III

VOLUME III

Prologue

"Loving you ain't nothing healthy."

-Vivian S. Greene,
Eric Roberson and Onsulade

Familiarity, Frustration, Contempt

I'm concerned that this love affair is a routine,
that the love is no longer there,
that you're here out of familiarity,
and our endless love has
become a mere affair.

I'm standing by,
living each day as it comes,
wondering where your heart is.
Does it still belong to me?
Am I still your Miss Lady
or is that all a memory?
I can't help but feel frustrated
and keep wanting more,
for I can't quite seem to understand
these damn feelings, I'm insecure.

Starting off so happily
each moment is so carefree

I'm foolishly blinded
by some childish fantasy.

Now, things don't seem quite the same.
Got a feeling that you're playing games.
Am I being paranoid?
Baby is it true?

I gotta know

'Cause I think, Baby, I'm not sure,
but I think I'm in Love with you.
I'm standing by,
living each day as it comes,
wondering where your heart is.
Does it still belong to me?
Starting off so happily,
each moment was so carefree.

Now things don't seem quite the same.
Oh, baby is it true?
I gotta know.
'Cause I think I'm in Love with you.

The Thin Line

I hate you,
I really do.
I hate you

times two.

I hate you,
because I love you,
and you love me so indifferently.

Trial and Error

Did your heart ever hurt
like mine does when I think of you?
Did your heart ever hurt?
Mine still skips a beat, no two.
Did your heart ever hurt?
Mine stands still with haunting memories of us two.

And I can't quite figure out
If I'm feeling this pain
'cause along the way I fell for you, or
because you don't even seem to love me anymore.
You don't even seem to care.
My presence doesn't seem to matter.
Do you still want me here?

Why am I insignificant?
Why don't you seem to care?
Am I destined to forever be lonely?
Did I once have a chance
at a fairy tale romance and foolishly
let it disappear?

Am I destined to never again know
the softness of his sweet embrace?
Am I fated to never be reacquainted
with his kisses?
Will I never know love again?
Oh, tell me it's not true.

Did your heart ever hurt
like mine does when I think of you?

I Think You Love Me

I think you love me.
Why else would you profess
the things you say
or refuse to let me walk away
and let me let my memories fade away?

I think you love me.
You seem to want to keep me
in sight 'till maybe that day arrives
when you wish to bid your scandalous ways
a good, good night.

I think you love me
like you once yelled in the middle of the street.
But at that moment
love did meet its defeat,
as you stood on the road
you weren't willing to travel
because your fragile heart was too weak.

I think you love me,
but that's not enough.

To think is to wonder,
To assume, to guess
Educated or not, this is not
a pop test.

I think you love me,
but you probably don't.
Love's a fact.
a known thing for true
for if you loved me
I'd know it, too.

Passive Resistant

I wish I could go back in time
and erase your past mistakes
that hinder your present happiness.

I wish I could turn back the hands of time
and lead you back on track,
when you began to go astray.

I wish I could kiss you on your lips
and make your misery melt away.

I wish I could have been a friend
on those painful days
when the pain was so unbearable
and the madness drove you crazy.
When the uncertainty kept you always wishing
and the wishing seemed unanswered.
When the misery made you lose hope
in the belief that you were worthy,
deserving of a smile in your heart, and
that you were allowed to be happy.

I wish I could hug you forever
and show you how much I care.
I wish that my love could enter your heart
and soothe all hurts away.

I wish that you found such comfort
in the embrace of my arms
that you'd allow me to be a lover and friend
and let your heart come alive again.

Masquerade

Duplicitous angels roam the earth
sometimes ordained in cherub face,
set with appeal of wicked smile,
a forked tongue,
and two sets of lips
whispering sonnets your heart has yearned to hear -
Sweet Nothings.
Pseudo sincerity, expressions laced with cunning charm.
False hope established on the foundation of empty promises.
Unleashing consecutive lures till guard is lowered.

Full of deceit and selfish charge,
suspending you at the threshold of appeasement
then, vanishes with no regard.

Reality

As I looked into his face,
I saw the truth that hope could not erase.

Affinity wasn't enough for either of us.
For with the events that reared us,
and the possibilities that fear consumed,
there simply wasn't an opportunity
for love to bloom.

Opposites attract,
Yes, that's true.
Chemistry draws you closer
almost like Krazy Glue.

And passion is the flame that keeps fantasies burning,
but never satisfies.
The unsatiated soul keeps yearning.

Duped

It's so true
we see what we want to see,
and hear what we want to hear
and hope that everything turns
out the way we fantasize about it.

But when we stop,
turn back the hands of time
replay the words we
camouflaged
beneath our desires,
and relive the situations past,
Clarity comes like a taunting voice
Whispering in your ear
and reality sets in.

Detour

You don't always get what you ask for,
and the prayers are answered in their own time.
And sometimes a wicked ear listens in
and sends a decoy to lead you astray,
misleading you with superficial
qualities that seem to answer that
knelt request.
Consumed in the pseudo companionship
that's nothing more than a little less
time all alone.

Spurts of affections, only as a Band Aid.
It's not sincere.
It's like the abuser who says I'm sorry,
but the bruise is already there.
Verbal abuse leaves a scar on the inside,
and emotional neglect may even be worse.

Why do you keep trying to squeeze love
out of heartless flesh?
That appreciation, courtesy, and respect you desire

isn't there for you
For reasons you'll never understand.
It's okay. Life's fucked up that way.
Life's not fair, and neither is love.

The spots are fixed,
The patterns don't change.
And the misery doesn't fade.

It simply becomes your luggage,
and even a backpack can weigh you down.

You don't always get what you ask for
but you keep what you settle for.

Detour – a longer, less clear, sometimes confusing, unsure way to your destination, and sometimes you get lost, before you find your way back on track.

Detour – continued

You follow the first detour
which is as clear as day.
You follow with momentary hesitation
and figure it has to be the way.

The route is unfamiliar,
your movements seem astray,
and with each uncertain turn
your assuredness seems to fade.

There comes a point when you seem to be vulnerable
in a place you just don't know.
Conflicted, and you don't know which way to go.

You second guess each action.
You're simply not sure anymore.
So, you haphazardly follow with uncertainty
and the journey now seems like a chore.
Your intended destination is quite clear
You're wondering how you got here,
each step taken with an element of fear.

You plan your move,
but then there's a fork.
You follow what seems to be going with the flow.
But then you feel to be taken for a ride,
led out to a place unknown.
Uncertain of what may happen,
what plan may lie ahead.

You decide that you can't continue this momentum,
and follow blindly anymore,
You come to your senses, assess the circumstance
and place your destiny in your own hands.

Why Do I Still Daydream About You?

Why do I still daydream about you?

I know we're over
no more me and you
but I can't stand this cleansing process
my mind is putting me through.
Every time I close my eyes
a short movie replays of us two.

I don't know why I still daydream about you.

I'm haunted by memories
where I refused to hear the clues
I was uncertain and confused,
wondering if those sweet accolades
were even true.

Why do I still daydream about you?
'Cause the daydreams stab me
as I relive the stress you put me through.

Daydream, no.
That's not true.
They're haunting memories.
You drew me in feeding me the sweetest nothings,
linking words together in ways I never knew
could be spouted
but behind the words laid admiration and contempt.
A foolish tug of war.
With growing resistance
you drew me into webs of confusion
that led to uncertainty.
My emotions began to brew.

I know why I'm still haunted by memories of you.
My heart's kind of lonely.
I'm feeling kind of blue
that's simply because no one's replaced
the spot once occupied by you.

Daydream – continued

I have such contempt for you.

You listened to me with wicked ear
and lied sonnets to me about things I love to hear.
A duplicitous angel is what you are,

a child of the master manipulator by far.
I can't hope that one day you'll meet your leader.
I'm having my own tug of war 'cause
you played with my heart at your leisure.
Your affection was always an appetite teaser.
Who gave you the right to take my vulnerable heart
and use it as your ego pleaser?

Malicious are all your deeds
and in your carelessness, you've produced a few seeds.
Your children's happiness can't be bought.
Hopefully love is easier on your daughter,
despite the actions of her father
Hopefully, no one takes her heart out to slaughter.

Remembering the Paperclip

- A Short Story -

There was a guy in my English class.
He used to sneak peeks at me, and I would pretend not to notice.
Finally, we got together on the pretense of sharing a book.
We worked on papers and grew closer together.

I remember one day we got into an argument over a true misunderstanding.

It ended that night and he walked out.
I should've gone after him.

The next day he returned with all of my
things that I had left in his room.
My pillow, some papers, my comb, a t-shirt,
my blue pen, and
a paperclip.
Not just another paperclip,
but mine.

My black plastic covered paperclip
that I had given to him for an English
assignment moments before it was due.

He Even Remembered the Paperclip.

Pure Love

Sometimes I just need to be held,
so I could bury my head and cry.

Some small gesture like a hug,
so my lonely heart won't die.

Reassure me that you care
and that you're appreciative that I'm here.

A simple embrace says so much, more than words
could ever do.

It's a simple soulful connection, a bond between two.

Weren't You There?

Weren't you there
when we first did meet,
when something about me, told something in you
that getting acquainted was a necessary deed?

Weren't you there
when we first did vibe?
A rendezvous at the Circle
and being entranced in the Big Square Time.

Weren't you there
when I first danced for you?
When we stood alone in
that crowded Time Square spot made for two.

Weren't you there
when we really first kissed
as you lay upon my floral bedspread?

Weren't you there
with me in Park Slope

when that girl stuffed her mouth at East Zen
and we thought she would choke?

Weren't you there At Highland Park
when I amazed you with pushups
and you flipped your way into my heart?

Weren't you there
for the days that didn't seem to end
when we cuddled and kissed, talked and laughed
and a closeness did seem to begin.

Weren't you there
when we got lost in Prospect Park?
When my fear had shown
and I clutched you close
as we entered a world unknown.

Weren't you there
when I felt that you took my feelings all for a joke?
So, you hopped on the Rail to express your care,
so I wouldn't feel like a dope.

Weren't you there
several times in your hood
when we talked for hours?
Didn't it feel good?

Weren't you there when our souls did dance
and trust was so real that we once took a taboo chance?

Weren't you there
with me at 1-2-5,
when I revealed past stories
and the true me you did vibe?

Weren't you there
In Washington Square Park,
when you twirled me and romanced me
into your heart, and
the sun sank slow,
and I gave you a made for one, gypsy dance show?

Weren't you there when I sat in my car,
and jumped to your rescue when I thought
the cops might be taking their power too far?

Weren't you there when I thought we were
seeing eye to eye, sharing a wavelength
and catching a vibe?
Weren't you there, or was it just me
when I thought we could share our thoughts
and mutual courtesy?

Yes, you were there, right there with me
relishing each day of our elusive, youthful fantasy.

SHIELDS

Who'd believe
that beneath my smile
there are pains that stretch
a thousand miles?

Who'd believe
that beneath my pleasant charm there were hurts and sorrows
so far gone?

Would you believe
the stories that my life has told,
a personal collection subtle, yet bold?
But what remains is a tattered soul.

Could you believe
a vulnerable heart with good intentions
from the very start could have been
so blind to life's turnabouts?
Never selfish, no doubts; would put an essence out to play if she'd known a better way.

I think not
and here I am
a disheartened child of so many - a man.

Hindsight

You know,

looking back,

I was just in love with the idea of being in love.

Volume IV

VOLUME IV

Prologue

"I wanna be your lover. I want to be the only one you come for."

-Prince

Chocolate

I love chocolate,
I love the way it melts in my mouth.
Milk Chocolate or Dark
that's what I'm talking 'bout.

I love chocolate kisses,
I love chocolate hugs.
I particularly like that chocolate
that's packaged just for one.

Chocolate flavored with coconut,
rerouted from the isles
is like a kiss of double flavored love
straight from paradise.

Now some of you ladies
may have had chocolate covered cherries.
Well, that's not my cup of tea,
give me chocolate covered nuts
and I'm in ecstasy.

I love chocolate,
the way it struts down the street,

dribbles a ball between his feet
and on the court, never meets defeat.

Give me chocolate,
short, medium or tall,
physically fit, with a six pack, and defined pecks,
cornrows, afro, caesar or bald.

Hmmm, give me some chocolate
with a pretty smile
juicy, full lips and a single gold tooth, set off to the side.

Educated chocolate,
gentlemen and street.
Articulate, and fun-loving,
and respectfully discreet.

Chocolate, chocolate, chocolate,
Chocolate I adore.
When I think I've had enough,
I keep coming back for more.

It's tempting, It's addictive,
It has an insatiable allure.

It's worse than a Lay's potato chip
it keeps you feenin' for more.

Anticipation

I long for your kiss
and yearn for you to kiss me.

I long to have your big strong hand
pull me to you.

I feen
for your lips to touch mine,
oh so soft and gentle
then open to receive my tongue
and to meet me halfway.
I swirl my tongue around yours
and you join in on the dance.
A merengue, I believe
as I plunge and engulf your tongue and massage it
with the walls
of my mouth pulling back oh so slightly and
methodically,
periodically slipping in a swirl, then returning to the
dance.

Lost in the intensity of your kiss and softness of your lips,
your hands palming my head, and
grasping my hair,
holding me steady as you melt into the love being
expressed.
Lost in our Utopia that lets me know
the depth of your passion,
Your love for me.
You pull back and look at me
heaved for breath,
provoked with titillations,
percolating within you.
Stirred by love you are now
willing to give
and be consumed by.

I long and yearn
for your kiss.

Did I say I long and yearn for your kiss?

I meant your dick.

Percolating

Part 1

I feel like I'm going to lose my mind
Waiting for you to
touch me.

I feel like I'm going to go insane
Waiting for you to
hold me
in your arms and embrace me
with your hands
cascading all over my body
charging me with anticipated ecstasy.

I want your hands all over my body.

Ravish Me

Part 2

I want your hands all over my body.

God forgive me.

I want to taste your tongue
after it's tasted my body.

I've sinned again.

I want to be engulfed within your arms,
solid and strong.
Take a bite into my neck
then soothe it with your lips and tongue.
Grab my head with both hands
lost in my hair as you
massage my tongue with your tongue
as our mouths get lost in a tango.

You provoke these thoughts within me,
and stir my innermost animal urges.

Grab my ass and pull me near
Lift me swiftly into the air,
Kiss them softly,
then kiss me there.

Flip me over,
oh, please do dare.
Ravish me baby,
don't you fear.
I'm percolating baby.
touch me there, touch me there.

Uhm, Baby you're a keeper, you're a gem.

Forgive me father
I've sinned again.

Penetration

I love the way you enter me
and fit yourself inside me, filling me up.
I love the way you sit there for a moment
and savor your home
then redecorate with personal touches.
First just engulfing yourself in its warmth,
getting yourself massagingly wet and lost.

Can you find your way back?

Having the day's worries melt away.
methodic and smooth,
each stroke more intense than the prior,
trying to reach new depths
you lose yourself between my thighs.

I love the way you reposition me
to feel new angles and spots unexplored,
inhibiting that pressure that builds inside
You, your loins.
Your manliness, I adore.
Inside my walls that you made wet,
saturated with the sweetest nectar,
creamy, wet
all for you.

A Glitch in My Main Frame

Hidden behind this mainframe,
And beyond the home page that lists
The miscellaneous info:
height, weight, complexion, length of mane,
personal style, glimmer of charm
and the presentation of name
is a malfunction with my program,
and a glitch in my mainframe.

Well, that's how a male platonic put it
while he was trying to figure out my game
that I used to select a mate.
He couldn't understand how I was drawn
to their bait.

Well, it's simple you see, opposites attract
isn't that true?
If I'm not mistaken, the girls you're drawn to
aren't anything like you.

"Yes", he replied, with a "what the hell is wrong with
you?" sigh

"You are too much of a lady,
too pretty, too cute
to mess around with the type of guy that
entices you."

I know, I know
It's a senseless tug of war
between what stimulates me, and what I need to settle
down.

What do you expect, me to be chaste?

For now, I'll take the former over the latter
until I come across an amalgamation
in the contradiction of my taste.

Volume V

VOLUME V

Prologue

"All I really want is to be happy,

to find a love that's mine.

It would be so sweet."

-Mary J. Blige
Sean Combs, Arlene DelValle,
and J.C. Oliver

Mystery Man

I can't wait to meet my husband.
I wonder who he might be.
How much patience must I have?
It's a frustrating mystery.

Will he be tall, dark and handsome,
or none of the above?
Will he be successful and rich?
Or will it be a marriage founded only on love?

Will he be educated or intelligent,
conversational or a bore?
Will he be the strong silent type
and know when to give a little tug of war?

Will he be forever occupied with his job,
consumed with his career?
Will he be obsessed with acquiring more wealth,
and in need of constant comfort from his peers?

Will he be kind and considerate,
respectful, attentive , well-rounded and
strong?

What will be my sacrifices?
What can I live without?

So many life experiences,
so much that I have learned
has made this a grave concern.

It's a Given

I want to be in love,
mutually.
Should I have not said that out loud?

Should I be ashamed to be needy
to not want to get around?

I want to be in love
Will that man, I ever find?

Should I be happy with my good health,
and content with peace of mind?

I want to be in love...
Is that too much to ask?

Is my request too demanding
too greedy to want more,
than sporadic outings and
casual sex?
Is monogamy truly a bore?

Should I try to fit in
and just be a whore?
Is to be in love
such an unnecessary chore?

I want to be in love
to vibe with one man,
to converse for endless hours
and spend silence with a friend.

I want to be in love
with a man that I can spoil,
and he share that honor, too.

I want to be in love,
Your Queen, your Goddess, ...I do.

I want to be in love.
Is that something that you can afford?

I want to be in love
and you be - my lord.

I want to be in love.

Should I have not said that out loud?

Confession and Prayer

Dear God,
I know I've been no angel,
errs, I've had a few,
but I don't understand this strife, my life's putting me through.

I think I'm being patient
and for the most part, a good girl.

Don't get me wrong,
I'm grateful for all your blessings.
Your bounties have been more than a few.
Your countless blessings, for those I am thankful,
but my love life has me singing the blues.

Is the tale truly a fairy?
Does happily ever after really come true?

When All Else Fails

God, please help me
to find a good man,
the ones that I attract,
are more than I can stand.

A man who's got style
that catches my eye,
and credentials on his resume
to make him worthwhile.

White collar, relaxed
blue collar, an entrepreneur.
Ambitious, a man with financial and career stability.
Success is quite an allure.

A man who doesn't mind cooking
for a woman he adores.
A man who doesn't think keeping things in order

are all a woman's chore.
A man who shows he's interested
by giving me his time.
A man who's not a player
that I can claim as all mine.

A man who's well rounded
who enjoys a variety of things.
Conversations on varied topics,
outgoing with periodic whims.

Picnics and novels lounging in the park
Chats over lattes cuddling up in the dark.

Periodic grinds on the dance floor,
each other, we adore.

Genuine, no gimmicks
Healthy, intelligent and brawn
and if I call him more than periodically
there's no cause for alarm.
It's simply means I'm digging him,
cause he's got captivating charm.
It means I find myself smiling
with a tingle in my heart.

Respect, adoration, God loving, courteous,
charismatic, monogamous, personable, and chivalrous

Passionate, a sense of humor, fun-loving, and witty
generous and good, with genuine sincerity

A man who enjoys kissing
and affection galore.

God, I await your blessing
so that my heart can soar.

I'd hate to throw in the towel
and admit that despair has won.
Nevertheless, not my will,
but Thine Will Be Done.

Waiting in Vain

Presented,
tempted, charmed
and provoked.

Chat: endless
Instant comfort-zone.

Pleasantly surprised.
Excited, optimistic, hopeful.

Smitten, maybe?

Waiting percolates.
Anticipation, calm.

The fruit dangled.
Informed; forbidden.
I dare not take a bite.

Disappointed, sad.
Possibilities; stifled.
Pleasures unexplored.

Out of sight, out of mind,
you learn how to put things into perspective.

However,
his presence; captivating
his stance; commanding

His smile; pleasant and beautiful,
full of life and love and
good intentions.
Sometimes it's his bashful charm.

Curiosity lingers.
Time passes.
Sincerity, unsure.

Doubts, yes.

*   *   *

Life continues and you wonder
What could have, would have been.
Time stands still for no one
and moments fade.

It's the could've, the didn't
that gets you every time.

Was it a detour or just a crooked path?
Missed possibilities because you were afraid to cross the line.

Demands? None.
Requests? I dare not.
Wonders? A few.
Intentions; clear.

I turn my attention to other things and
wait for that butterfly to come sit softly on my shoulder.

Epilogue
A Love Story

A Love Affair
that had long ago, gone sour
and lay dormant from pride and principle,
stood timeless
while the outsiders watched idly by
at a pair of singles who coupled with no one else.

A chance rendezvous? No.
She had usually laid them out quite coincidentally.

Time: the greatest healer, or tormentor, or even yet the
most profound teacher haunts you with realizations
and taunts you with flashes of her smile, and
all the wondrous expressions that came
most unexpectedly – especially – only for you.
He swallows - and orchestrates a chance encounter.

They, as friends
under the cozy conditions,
keep conversation as unemotional as possible,
as new entranced probable mates.

Each remark laced with the simplicity of
its expression is heaved with
bated expectation.
He's beguiled by her like the first moment
he laid his eyes on her.

She's anticipatory of the affirmation that
he could never quite express so many Blue Moons ago.
He's smitten and overwhelmed by all the
inner beauty he had refused to succumb to
due to his youthful trysts.

Her disappointments restrain the emotions
that caress the heart of her soul.

The paranoia of possible pain
that she could cause his heart
makes her hesitant and cautious of each word that she's
compelled to impart, and he too.

The chat was quite endless.
Interrupted by bouts of silence.

Mesmerized by the possibility
with contemplations of their destiny.

As the *'vous'* came to an end,
he brushes her hair from her face
cascades his fingers across her cheeks to
the back of her mane.
He moves in with the most ravishing intent
and places his mouth so soft but intense
and kisses her deeply with a yearning embrace.
Hands lost in the tresses of her head.

Their lips part, eyes peering
as the smirks on their faces read
'Here we go again'.

Conclusion
Who I Am

"Now I lay me down to sleep
I pray The Lord my Soul to keep
If I should die before I wake
I pray the Lord my soul to take" *

I'm afraid to go to sleep
because I haven't said goodbye
but I'm afraid that if I do
that that will seal my fate.

I'm afraid to close my eyes
to rest my sorrowed soul
to drift off into uncharted lands
No, I couldn't be so bold.

I'm afraid that if I rest my spirit
that she may drift away
to a land thought of free from worries
pain and misery.

And even so,
I haven't quite lived life
I haven't given birth to twins
or been taken for a wife.

I'm afraid to close my heavy eyes
to kiss the day good night
For I haven't yet
finished writing my books, planted a tree, become a
famous movie star or
set all caged animals free.

I'm still afraid to go to sleep
for you see this little girl
with all my plans and woes,
has yet to save the world.

* Sidney D. Mitchell and George W. Meyer

Index

Questions for Discussion

1. Do you think the prologue quotes accurately encapsulated the volume they introduced?

2. Which poem resonated with you, evoked memories?

3. Which poem is your favorite, and why?

4. Was the scenario/man in "Waiting in Vain" a detour or a crooked path, and thus a missed opportunity?

5. Who do you think is being referred to in the poem, "A Love Story"?

6. Do you agree with Henry David Thoreau, in the Epigraph quote "Happiness", that love will come when you're not pursuing it?